The Five Mile Press Pty. Ltd.
67 Rushdale Street
Knoxfield Victoria 3180 Australia

First published 1991
This paperback edition first published 1992
Copyright © Shirley Barber
Design by Geoff Hocking

Typeset by DigiType, Bendigo
Printed in Hong Kong by South China Printing Company (1988) Limited

Barber, Shirley.
Daphne, the Forgetful Duck

ISBN 0 86788 463 0

1. Ducks – Juvenile fiction. I. Title.

A823.3

They told the old herb woman the whole story.

When it was finished, she said to Daphne, "The only reason you lost your ducklings is because your memory is so bad. Try my very special herbal tonic — it will soon make your memory much better."

And so it did! After that, Daphne always remembered to leave her ducklings at the apple-tree house on market morning. And the three friends went to market after lunch.

William and the ducklings became great friends, and Daphne never had to worry about her bad memory again.

At last, the boat reached the apple-tree house.
How happy Daphne was to see her ducklings safe!